My Very First
PRAYERS

Compiled by Juliet David
Illustrations by Helen Prole

Copyright © 2015 Lion Hudson/Tim Dowley Associates

All rights reserved. No part of this publication may be reproduced or transmitted in any form or by any means, electronic or mechanical, including photocopy, recording, or any information storage and retrieval system, without permission in writing from the publisher.

Published by Candle Books
an imprint of
Lion Hudson plc
Wilkinson House, Jordan Hill Road,
Oxford OX2 8DR, England
www.lionhudson.com/candle

ISBN 978 1 78128 170 3
e-ISBN 978 1 78128 195 6

First edition 2010
This edition 2015

A catalogue record for this book is available from the British Library

Printed and bound in China, April 2016, LH06

My Very First PRAYERS

Compiled by Juliet David
Illustrations by Helen Prole

CANDLE BOOKS

Contents

The Lord's Prayer. 7

Good Morning! 8

Mealtimes. 9

Prayer Time 11

Today!. 14

Me, Myself, and I. 15

Jesus Our Friend. 20

All the People I Love 21

Sorry! 24

All Things Bright and Beautiful 25

Christmas 28

Easter 29

Harvest 30

Thank You! 31

Sweet Dreams 32

While We Sleep 36

Praise him, praise him
Everybody praise him –
God is love, God is love!

The Lord's Prayer

Our Father in heaven,
hallowed be your name,
your kingdom come,
your will be done,
on earth as in heaven.
Give us today our daily bread.
Forgive us our sins
as we forgive those who sin against us.
Lead us not into temptation
but deliver us from evil.
For the kingdom, the power,
and the glory are yours
now and forever.
Amen

Good Morning!

Thank you, God in heaven,
For a day begun.
Thank you for the breezes,
Thank you for the sun.

Mealtimes

Thank you for the world so sweet,
Thank you for the food we eat,
Thank you for the birds that sing,
Thank you, God, for everything.

For health and strength
and daily food,
we praise your name,
O Lord.

Prayer Time

Hush little puppy
　with your *bow, wow, wow*.
Hush little kitty
　with your *meow, meow, meow*.
Hush Mr Rooster
　with your *cock-a-doodle-doo*.
Please don't *moo-moo*, Mrs Cow.
Hush, hush, hush!
Hush, hush, hush!
Somebody's talking to God right now.

This is the church,
And this is the steeple
Open the doors
And see all the people!
Close the doors
And the people all pray.

God, make my life a little light
Within the world to glow;
A little flame that burns so bright
Wherever I may go.

Today!

Keep my little tongue today,
Make it kind while I play;
Keep my hands from doing wrong,
Guide my feet the whole day long.
Amen

Me, Myself, and I

Jesus, friend of little children,
Be a friend to me;
Take my hand and ever keep me,
Close to thee.

God made the sun,
And God made the trees,
God made the mountains,
And God made me.

Thank you, God,
For the sun and the trees,
For making the mountains,
And for making me.

Two little eyes to look to God;
Two little ears to hear his word;
Two little feet to walk in his ways;
Two little lips to sing his praise;
Two little hands to do his will
And one little heart to love him still.

The Lord is my shepherd;
I have everything I need.
He lets me rest
in fields of green grass
and leads me
to quiet pools of fresh water.

Give me joy in my heart,
Keep me praising,
Give me joy in my heart, I pray.
Give me joy in my heart,
Keep me praising –
Keep me praising
Till the break of day.

Jesus Our Friend

Jesus bids us shine
With a pure, clear light,
Like a little candle
Burning in the night;
In this world of darkness,
So we must shine,
You in your small corner,
And I in mine.

All the People I Love

Bless this house, O Lord we pray,
Make it safe by night and day;
Bless these walls so firm and stout,
Keeping want and trouble out.

Bless the roof and chimneys tall,
Let thy peace lie over all;
Bless this door, that it may prove
ever open to joy and love.

Father God,
Thank you for my family –
not just those who live with us,
but grandparents, uncles, aunts,
and cousins.
Please be with all of them today.
Amen

Dear God,
Please love me,
Take care of me,
Bless me.

Please love my sister,
Take care of her,
Bless her.

Please love my brother,
Take care of him,
Bless him.

Sorry!

God, you are great.
You made the world – and it's good.
Thank you for making it so beautiful.
We're sorry we've spoiled it.
Amen

All Things Bright and Beautiful

For air and sunshine, pure and sweet,
We thank our heavenly Father;
For grass that grows beneath our feet,
We thank our heavenly Father.

Dear Lord,
Today we went to the zoo.
We saw lots of animals:
Giant elephants, tiny lizards,
Chattering monkeys, gentle deer.
You made them all,
Big and small.
Thank you.

God, who made the earth,
The air, the sky, the sea,
Who gave the light its birth,
Careth for me.

God, who made the grass,
The flower, the fruit, the tree,
The day and night to pass,
Careth for me.

Christmas

Away in a manger
No crib for a bed,
The little Lord Jesus
Laid down his sweet head.

The stars in the bright sky
Looked down where he lay
The little Lord Jesus
Asleep in the hay.

Easter

There is a green hill far away,
Outside a city wall,
Where the dear Lord was crucified
Who died to save us all.

Jesus Christ is risen today.
Alleluia!

Harvest

All good gifts around us
Are sent from heaven above.
Then thank the Lord,
O thank the Lord,
For all his love.

Thank You!

Thank you, God,
For the sun and the trees.
For wonderful flowers
And buzzing bees.

For the sounds I hear
And the sights I see,
But most of all, thank you
For making me *me*!

Sweet Dreams

Bless us in the morning,
Bless us through the day,
Bless us as we go to sleep,
And keep us safe, we pray.

Jesus, tender Shepherd, hear me,
Bless your little lamb tonight;
Through the darkness please be near me,
Keep me safe till morning light.

I see the moon,
The moon sees me:
God bless the moon,
And God bless me.

Be near me, Lord Jesus,
I ask you to stay
Close by me forever
And love me, I pray.

Bless all the dear children
In your tender care
And take us to heaven
To live with you there.

While We Sleep

Dear God,
Sometimes I wake up in the night
   and feel a bit scared.
Help me to remember
   that you are always with me.
Then I won't need to be afraid.

Matthew, Mark,
   Luke, and John,
Bless the bed
   that I lie on.

Index of First Lines

All good gifts around us *Matthias Claudius (1740–1815)* 30
Away in a manger *Anonymous* 28
Be near me, Lord Jesus *Anonymous* 35
Bless this house, O Lord we pray *Helen Taylor* 21
Bless us in the morning 32
Dear God, Please love me 23
Dear God, Sometimes I wake up in the night 36
Dear Lord, Today we went to the zoo 26
Father God, Thank you for my family 22
For air and sunshine, pure and sweet *Traditional* 25
For health and strength *Traditional* 10
Give me joy in my heart *Traditional* 19
God made the sun 16
God, make my life a little light *Matilda Betham-Edwards (1836–1919)* 13
God, who made the earth *Sarah Betts Rhodes (c. 1870)* 27
God, you are great 24
Hush little puppy *Traditional* 11
I see the moon *Traditional* 34
Jesus bids us shine *Anonymous* 20
Jesus Christ is risen today 29
Jesus, friend of little children *Walter J. Mathams (1853–1931)* 15
Jesus, tender Shepherd, hear me *Mary L. Duncan (1814–40)* 33
Keep my little tongue today 14
Matthew, Mark, Luke, and John *Traditional* 37
Our Father in heaven 7
Praise him, praise him *Traditional* 6
Thank you for the world so sweet *E. Rutter Leatham* 9
Thank you, God 31

Thank you, God in heaven *Traditional* 8
The Lord is my shepherd 18
There is a green hill far away *Mrs C. F. Alexander* 29
This is the church 12
Two little eyes to look to God *Colin C. Kerr* 17

Acknowledgments

The Lord's Prayer (page 7) from Common Worship: Services and Prayers for the Church of England (Church House Publishing, 2000) is copyright © The English Language Liturgical Consultation, 1988 and is reproduced by permission of the publisher.

"Two little eyes to look to God" (page 17) copyright © Mr Ian Kerr www.ebtrust.org.uk

Psalm 23:1–2 (page 18) is taken from the Good News Bible © 1994 published by the Bible Societies/HarperCollins Publishers Ltd UK, Good News Bible © American Bible Society 1966, 1971, 1976, 1992. Used with permission.

Every effort has been made to trace and contact copyright owners.
We apologize for any inadvertent omissions or errors.